To little Mérédith
—Louis Joos

For my brother, Stephen
—Rascal

Library of Congress Cataloging-in-Publication Data

Rascal.
Oregon's journey / by Rascal; pictures by Louis Joos.
p.   cm.
Summary: Duke, a circus dwarf, takes Oregon, a circus bear, back
home to Oregon.
ISBN 0-8167-3305-8 (lib. bdg.)   ISBN 0-8167-3306-6 (pbk.)
[1. Circus—Fiction.   2. Bears—Fiction.   3. Voyages and travels—
Fiction.]   I. Joos, Louis, ill.   II. Title.
PZ7.R18147Or   1994
[E]—dc20   93-11796

OREGON'S JOURNEY

by RASCAL • pictures by LOUIS JOOS

BridgeWater Books

We met at a circus in Pittsburgh, Oregon and I.
Watching him from behind the red curtain,
I felt like a child again.

DUKE the star of the clowns!

After my performance, I would walk him back
to his cage.
One evening, Oregon spoke to me.
"Take me to the big forest, Duke."
At first, I did not know what to say.

But back in my trailer,
I knew that Oregon should be among other bears,
deep in a beautiful forest of spruce trees.
Perhaps there, I, a dwarf, might meet Snow White.

When the final performance was over,
we walked out into the dark night.
We had no luggage,
nor any need for pocket-bulging keys.

I looked around and guessed that the big forests,
with pine trees and rivers full of fish,
were not nearby. We had to move on.

Miles later, Pittsburgh and its ash-colored sky
were far in the past.

We bought two one-way tickets to Chicago.
Three hundred hamburgers later, my savings were gone.
But I didn't mind. I was happy to make this journey
with Oregon.

At dawn, we hitched a ride with a man heading to Iowa.
He said he was on his way to America's breadbasket.
Just talking about food made Oregon hungry.

"Why do you wear white makeup and a red nose
when you're no longer in the circus?" the man asked me.
"Because they've become a part of me," I answered.
"It isn't easy being a dwarf."

"Nor is it easy to be a black man," he said.
We understood each other.

We parted in the morning. I had a promise to keep,
and there was still a long way to go.

My red hair blowing in the wind,
I went through landscapes as beautiful as
van Gogh's paintings.

We walked through hail.
We snacked in corn fields.
We snoozed in the warm grass.
We dreamed under the stars.
The birds were our alarm clock,
the streams our baths.
The whole world belonged to us.

Carried by the wind of the Great Plains,
with sore feet and my thumb pointed to the sky,
we were on our way to the Rocky Mountains.

A traveling salesman, a hopeful actress, and a Navajo elder took us farther on our way.
But at dusk, we were so exhausted that all we could do was sleep.
We spent the night in an old, abandoned Chevrolet.

First thing in the morning, we hopped on a moving
train to finish the last leg of our trip.
With Oregon as a pillow,
I dozed off, watching the cows go by.

When I woke up, there it was!

With just a few steps,
Oregon forgot all his years in captivity.

Oregon in Oregon! I had kept my promise.

I walked into the white morning,
light at heart, and happy.